Cinderella

ORCHARD

For Ismene Catchpole U.J.
For my little sister Lydia J.C.T.

ORCHARD BOOKS

First published in Great Britain in 2018

by The Watts Publishing Group

First published in paperback in 2019

1 3 5 7 9 10 8 6 4 2

Text © Ursula Jones 2018

Illustrations © Jessica Courtney Tickle 2018

The moral rights of the author and illustrator have been asserted.

All rights reserved.

A CIP catalogue record for this book is available from the British Library.

ISBN 978 1 40834 570 2

Printed and bound in China

Orchard Books

An imprint of Hachette Children's Group

Part of The Watts Publishing Group Limited

Carmelite House, 50 Victoria Embankment, London EC4Y 0DZ

An Hachette UK Company

www.hachette.co.uk

www.hachettechildrens.co.uk

Cinderella

Ursula Jones
Jessica Courtney Tickle

ORCHARD

Once upon a time there was a man who had a daughter. She was as kind and beautiful as her mother had been.

One day, the man brought home a haughty-looking bride with two grumpy bridesmaids trudging behind her.

"This is my new wife and her sweet girls," he told his daughter. "They will be a loving stepmother and stepsisters to you."

But they weren't. They were horrible.

At the wedding feast, the elder stepsister whispered to the younger, "Don't sit next to that daughter of his. She's so pretty she makes you look ugly."

"Not as ugly as you," hissed her sister, and they made the daughter sit at the far end of the table.

At bedtime, the stepsisters
barged into her room.
"Push-off, Miss Too-Pretty-By
Half," said the elder sister.
"This is our bedroom."
The stepmother took her up to the attic.
"You sleep here now," she said and
shut the door on her.

It was so dark and so cold that she tiptoed down to
the kitchen fire in the basement. Buttons, the little
dog whose job it was to chase away the rats, was
asleep in the warm embers. He gave her a friendly lick
as she crept in beside him and lay down in the cinders.
"They're just tired after the wedding," she told him.
"You'll see, Buttons, they'll turn out to be very nice."
After ten years at a Charm School, thought Buttons.
"They'll be different in the morning," she said.
And I'll be a flying hot dog, thought Buttons.

And they weren't different.

"Good morning, Miss Ashbum," laughed the elder stepsister when she saw she'd been sitting in the ash.

"Hello, Cinder-Rear," jeered the younger.

The stepmother gave her a crust and sent her to the cellars.

"You're too cindery to eat breakfast with us," she said.

"Cinders in the cellar," sneered her stepsisters. "Cinder-cellar, Cinderella!"

And the name stuck.

Cinderella fed the crust to the mice in the cage-traps her stepmother had set.

"Cheer up," she said. "Things will change." And things did: they got worse.

Her stepmother was angry with Cinderella because she was prettier than her own daughters. She made her do all the housework and cooking and dig the vegetable garden while the spotty stepsisters lounged about, sucking sweets and shouting orders. Cinderella's dress got torn and dirty and her shoes wore thin running errands for her stepsisters.

If ever Cinderella's father asked where she was,
her stepmother said, "Out enjoying herself."
"No, she's not," Buttons would shout. "Look down here,
you love-struck poodle, she's scrubbing the doorstep,
corgi brain." But it only came out as a bark.

One day, the king's son asked everyone to a ball. The stepsisters
were so excited when Cinderella brought them the prince's invitation,
the elder sister choked on her sweet. She turned bright puce.
"See what you've done, Cinderella," the younger sister scolded.
"Now she'll look like a beetroot in a ball gown at the prince's party!"
"Who are you calling a beetroot, Banana Nose?" snarled her sister, and
their mother had to separate them before they pulled out each other's hair.

Then dressmakers sewed the stepsisters' new frocks, kilos of makeup
were bought, and enough perfume to fill a bathtub.

The great day arrived.

"Do our hair, Cinderella," commanded the stepsisters.

"Put on our makeup. Make us beautiful."

And Cinderella, who was as clever as she was kind, did. Well, sort of.

"Why don't you come to the ball too, Cinderella?" the younger sister asked.

"How could I, dressed like this?" sighed Cinderella.

"We could lend you a gown," grinned the elder sister.

"But we won't," laughed the younger sister. And away they went to the ball.

Cinderella sat by the kitchen fire and, for the first time, she cried. The fire sputtered and spat as her tears fell on the flames. Then, with a flurry of sparks, a fiery-looking person swooped out of the chimney.

"Your tears," snapped the fairy, "are putting out my fire."

"Sorry," wept Cinderella. "But I so want to go to the ball."

"What's stopping you?" demanded the fiery fairy.

"I haven't got anything to go in."

"Is that all!" exclaimed the fairy. "Fetch me a pumpkin."

Cinderella ran to the vegetable garden. Perhaps she's going to make pumpkin soup, she thought, as she brought back the pumpkin.

"You got mice?" asked the fiery fairy.

"I'm afraid so," said Cinderella.

"Fetch them."

She's surely not going to put mice in her soup, thought Cinderella.

"Now bring me the six lizards asleep behind the watering cans."

"This is going to be the most terrible soup," Cinderella said to herself as she obeyed.

"Got a rat?" asked the fairy.

"Not one," said Cinderella. "Thanks to Buttons."

"He'll do," said the fiery fairy.

"Oh, no!" begged Cinderella. "Please don't cook Buttons."

"I'm no cook," said the fiery fairy, producing her wand. "I'm your fairy godmother."

"Phew!" barked Buttons.

She tapped the pumpkin
with the wand.

Flash! Boing!

It turned into a golden coach.

Tap

went the wand on the mouse
cage. With a flash, a squeak and
a whinny, the mice became four
smart horses to draw the coach.

Tap

went the wand on the bucket, and
the lizards turned into six spruce
footmen – still snoozing.
"Show a leg, boys," said the fairy
godmother. And the footmen
leapt on to the coach.

"Now all we need is a driver," said the fairy godmother. **Tap** went the wand and Buttons was suddenly a coachman. "I can talk," he said, cracking his whip. "But it's a dog's life, I can't think what to say." "Try 'gee-up' for starters," suggested the fairy godmother. She pointed at the coach. "There you are, Cinderella. Now you've got something to go to the ball in."

"Thank you, Fairy Godmother," cried Cinderella. "But I need to change."

"Into what?" asked the fairy, raising her wand.

"I mean from my dirty clothes," Cinderella said quickly, before she got changed into the spare wheel.

Tap

went the wand. With a flash and a silvery-sounding twiddle, Cinderella's grubby dress had vanished. There she stood, in the most beautiful swirling, shimmering ball gown ever made.

"How perfect!" she gasped.

"Not bad," agreed her fairy godmother, "but the shoes could be classier."

Tap ⸱ Flash ⸱ Ping

And Cinderella was wearing the prettiest little pair of sparkling glass slippers.

"Have a good time," cried her fairy godmother as the footmen helped Cinderella into the coach. "But be sure to leave before midnight. At midnight the magic will run out."

"I'll remember," Cinderella promised, blowing her a kiss.

"Up-gee," shouted Buttons, and away went Cinderella to the ball.

The prince was having fun at his ball when he was told a latecomer had turned up. He was a polite prince, so he went to welcome them. And was he glad he had! Stepping out of her coach was the loveliest princess he had ever seen. He bowed.

"May I escort you into the ball?"

"Thank you," replied Cinderella. "I was wondering where it was."

When they arrived, everything stopped.
Nobody danced, nobody spoke or laughed
or even coughed. The band forgot to play.
They were all so dazzled by the radiant
princess. Then the prince asked
Cinderella to dance. And as they
danced and talked and laughed
the night away, the prince fell
head over heels in love with her.

But suddenly the palace clock began to chime the strokes of midnight.

One "Oh!" remembered Cinderella.

Two "I must go."

Three "Goodbye, Prince."

Four "Thank you."

Five She ran through the dancers.

Six Up the staircase,

Seven, Eight along the corridors.

Nine She reached the door.

Ten She ran down the steps to where her coach was waiting.

Eleven The footmen flung open the coach door.

Twelve!

"Too late. The magic's over!" barked Buttons the Coachman as he turned back into a dog. The mice ran off to the pantry, the lizards went to sleep under the steps, the pumpkin turned to squish and Cinderella and Buttons pelted home.

By the time the prince reached the door, they had disappeared. The prince was very unhappy to lose the girl he loved. Then he saw a little glass slipper lying on the steps where it had fallen off Cinderella's foot. And that gave him an idea.

Cinderella and Buttons snuggled into the embers. "I've had a wonderful time," Cinderella said sleepily. "Thank you, Fairy Godmother."

Next afternoon, the stepsisters were still in their dressing gowns when a procession of courtiers trooped in, carrying the little glass slipper.

"The prince says every lady in the land is to try on this slipper," one proclaimed. "Whoever it fits, he will ask to be his wife."

"Me first," shouted the elder sister.

"Good luck," said the courtier wearily. "Four hundred grand ladies have already failed."

The elder stepsister pushed her foot into the slipper. But she could only fit in her big toe.

"Push harder, Fat-Foot," her mother ranted. But the slipper was far too small. The elder stepsister wept with rage.

"My turn," smiled the youngest. "I'm a natural royal." But although she nearly broke her toes with squeezing, her heel still stuck out of the back of the slipper.

"Too bad," sighed the courtier, who'd been enjoying a sit-down. "Off we go again."

"Call Cinderella," Buttons entreated the father. "Give Cinderella a chance."
But it only came out as a bark. Nothing for it, thought Buttons.
This will do the trick. And he peed against a stepsister.
What a rumpus! The stepsister squawked, the courtiers
jumped clear, the father shouted, "No dinner for you," and
the stepmother screamed, "Cinderella, come and mop up!"
No dinner but a winner, thought Buttons as Cinderella arrived
in her filthy dress and asked, "May I try on the slipper?"

"No!" screeched the stepmother. But the courtier said he didn't see why not. So Cinderella tried on the slipper.

"It fits,"

chorused the courtiers. "And here is the other one," said Cinderella, taking it from her pocket.

Floof went the fire in the grate. There stood the fiery fairy godmother. With one tap of her wand, Cinderella was wearing the loveliest dress yet, and everyone recognized the beautiful princess from the ball. The stepmother and sisters fainted on to the father to get themselves out of trouble. But it didn't work. The fairy godmother was about to change them all into puddles of goo when the prince came in and asked Cinderella to marry him. Everyone was so happy, they forgot about the awful sisters.

Cinderella and her prince had a sumptuous wedding. Buttons was
made a lord, and went to live in the palace with the newly-weds.
Now this is what you call a dog's life, thought Lord Buttons.

∽ The End ∽